SKATING
Showdown

BY JAKE MADDOX

text by Margaret Gurevich
illustrated by Katie Wood

STONE ARCH BOOKS
a capstone imprint

Jake Maddox books are published by Stone Arch Books
A Capstone Imprint
1710 Roe Crest Drive
North Mankato, Minnesota 56003
www.capstonepub.com

Library of Congress Cataloging-in-Publication Data is available on
the Library of Congress website.

Summary: With a big figure skating competition coming up, Grace
has to remember why she loved skating in the first place.

ISBN 978-1-4342-4012-5 (library binding)
ISBN 978-1-4342-4204-4 (pbk.)

Designer: Kristi Carlson
Production Specialist: Laura Manthe

Printed in China by Nordica.
1012/CA21201278
092012   006935NORDS13

TABLE OF CONTENTS

Chapter One

ENTERING THE COMPETITION

Grace tried not to yawn as she leaned down to lace up her skates before stepping onto the ice. Waking up early for morning practice wasn't easy. But when she hit the ice, she was immediately energized.

Coach Roberts was running late, and Grace was excited to have the rink to herself for a few minutes. First she warmed up without her music. She pushed off with her right foot, then her left, skating smoothly across the ice.

Once her leg muscles felt loose, Grace raised one foot off the ice and practiced gliding on the opposite foot.

I can't believe how hard this move seemed when I first started skating, Grace thought. *It seems like forever ago.*

Grace closed her eyes as she glided with both feet on the ice. She heard clapping behind her and turned to see Coach Roberts standing off to the side watching.

"I see you're already warming up," Coach Roberts said with a smile. "You're my most dedicated skater."

Grace smiled. "Thanks," she said. "I was just thinking about how hard this used to be." She stepped off of the ice and pulled on her skate guards. Then she walked over and joined her coach on a bench.

Coach Roberts smiled. "You've definitely come a long way," he agreed. "Which is why I think you'd be perfect for this." He reached into his pocket and pulled out a folded piece of paper.

Grace saw the words YOUTH EXHIBITION AND COMPETITION printed across the top of the paper. Her heart jumped with excitement. She'd been in exhibitions before but never a competition.

"I've been thinking for a while now that we should enter you in a competition, and this one is right in River City," Coach Roberts said. "I think you could do really well in it."

Grace grinned. The idea of competing scared her, but it was also thrilling. *At least it will give me something to work toward,* she thought.

Grace jumped up from the bench. "Let's get going," she said. "I already warmed up."

Coach Roberts laughed. "Okay, settle down," he said. "I know you're excited to get started, but let's go over the competition requirements first." He smoothed out the competition flier and scanned it as Grace impatiently shuffled her skates. "Since spins are your strength, let's start your routine with a pivot," he suggested.

"Sounds good," Grace said, grinning. She loved doing spins. They always made her feel so graceful and elegant.

Grace stepped onto the ice and skated to the center of the rink to get into position. She placed the toe pick of her left blade into the ice and pushed off with her right foot. Then she pivoted around her left foot.

"Great job, Grace!" Coach Roberts called.

"Thanks," said Grace. "Too bad we have to include jumps too."

Coach Roberts laughed. "I know you can do it," he said.

Grace appreciated her coach's confidence in her. She knew she could do the jumps, but they weren't her best moves. She was much better at spins.

"Let's start out with a mohawk sequence," Coach Roberts said. "It will build off of the mohawk turn you learned when you first started skating. I'll walk you through it."

"Okay," Grace said, nodding. The mohawk turn was a pretty basic move. It let a skater easily change direction by shifting weight from one foot to the other.

"Start on your left foot, and do a crossover," Coach Roberts said.

Grace started skating around the curve of the rink on her left outside edge. Then she crossed her right foot over her left and transferred her weight to her right inside edge. She crossed her feet again coming out of the turn, finishing on her left outside edge.

"Very good!" her coach called. "Now go into a mohawk turn. With the mohawk you'll be changing feet, but not your edge. Start with your feet in a T position."

Grace made her right foot the top of the T and held her balance. She always needed patience to learn a new move.

I just want to get going already, Grace thought impatiently.

"Now push off with the left foot, so you're stroking away from your right foot," Coach Roberts instructed.

Grace put her arms out for balance and glided forward on the inside edge of her skate. She kept her other foot lifted off the ice.

"Nice," her coach said. "Now pull your left heel in close to the inside of your right foot. Careful not to touch the ice! Great! Don't forget to keep gliding on your right foot." Coach Roberts mimicked the steps with his own feet so Grace could see the movements more clearly.

Grace brought her left foot up next to her right skate and turned it out at a 90-degree angle. The heel of her left skate was centered in the middle of her right.

"We're almost done," Coach Roberts said. "Now, put your left skate down onto the ice, and pick your right foot up at the same time. Transfer your weight to your left foot and glide back with it."

Grace placed her left foot down on the ice and shifted her weight to her left leg. She bent her right knee and lifted her foot off the ice. Turning her body to face her foot, Grace glided backward on the inside edge of her skate.

"Perfect!" Coach Roberts called. "Now put it all together and keep shifting the weight from one foot to the other."

Grace spent the rest of the practice working on the mohawk sequence. She had the start of her routine down. By the time practice ended, she was glowing.

"Feels good to master something new, doesn't it?" her coach asked.

"Definitely!" said Grace. "I can't wait to do more!"

Coach Roberts laughed. "Keep up that attitude, and you'll do great at the competition," he told her.

* * *

That night at dinner, Grace was too excited to eat. "Coach Roberts wants me to enter the skating competition in River City!" she told her parents. "The winner gets a medal and her name on a plaque in the town hall. Coach really thinks I could win."

"That's great news," Grace's mom replied. She pointed to Grace's untouched pasta. "But don't forget to eat, or you won't have energy to compete."

Grace sighed and shoved a forkful of spaghetti into her mouth.

"I saw a poster downtown about that competition," Grace's dad said. "It's part of the River City Winter Festival. It sounds like it will be fun."

"I can't wait!" Grace exclaimed.

Grace's mom smiled and pointed to the plate again. "Energy," she reminded Grace.

"Plus I learned a new turn sequence today," Grace said, taking a bite of her pasta. "Coach said if I keep practicing, I'll definitely have a shot at a medal."

"That's good to hear," her dad said. "But don't forget to have fun too."

Grace laughed. *How could I not have fun?* she thought. *Skating is my favorite thing to do.*

Chapter Two

AN INTIMIDATING PRACTICE

The next morning, Grace woke up early, as usual, but she wasn't tired at all.

I can't wait to get to the rink and practice, she thought. *I need to spend as much time on the ice as possible before the competition.*

Coach Roberts was waiting for her when she arrived. He was standing next to an older woman and a girl about Grace's age. The girl was wearing skating gear. Coach Roberts spotted Grace and waved her over.

"Grace, I want you to meet someone," he said. He motioned to the girl standing next to him. "This is Lauren. She's going to be competing in the River City Skating Competition, too. And this is her coach, Patricia. She and I used to skate together."

"Nice to meet you both," said Grace. But she couldn't help worrying. *What if she's better than I am?* Grace thought.

"You too," Lauren said. "I just transferred to River City. It's nice to meet another skater. Maybe we can practice together sometime. It would be fun to help motivate each other."

Grace wasn't sure she wanted to practice with someone she'd be competing against, but she kept smiling anyway. She didn't want to be a downer. "Sure," she said. "Sounds good."

"Well, we'd better get started," Patricia said. "Have a good practice." With that, she and Lauren turned and walked to one of the other rinks to practice. Grace and Coach Roberts walked to their ice.

"Let's warm up with backward glides and swizzles today," Coach Roberts suggested.

Grace nodded and headed to the bench. She slipped off her skate guards and stored them in her bag before heading to the rink.

As she stepped onto the ice, Grace bent her knees and straightened her torso. Then she lifted her chin and held her arms out in front of her. She pushed back on her toes for the glide, then transferred her weight onto the heel of her skate to move backward.

"Remember the fish!" Coach Roberts called.

Grace smiled. That's how she'd learned to do the backward swizzles when she first started skating. She imagined her feet making fish patterns in the ice. She picked up speed looping around the rink.

Coach Roberts clapped. "Nice work," he called. "Now let's try a combination. Forward and backward glides and swizzles."

Grace spread her arms wide. She crisscrossed her feet as she skated around the rink. She made sure to check behind her on the swizzles, too.

Everything is coming together, Grace thought. She slowed down to catch her breath.

"Fantastic! Next we'll try our spins. First the two-foot spin, then the one-foot. Sound good?" Coach Roberts asked.

"Perfect!" said Grace. Spins were her best moves.

Coach Roberts turned on the music for her routine, and Grace skated across the ice. She picked up speed in time to the music, moving faster and faster.

When it was time for her spin, Grace circled her arms out in front of her like she was holding a beach ball. As she spun, she drew her arms tightly into her chest. She spun on the ice, lifting one leg up. Then she put her leg down and tucked her arms in tighter. In this position, she could turn even faster. Grace imagined herself spinning off the ice.

"Bravo!" Coach Roberts cheered. "Spins are definitely your signature move."

Grace grinned. "Thanks," she replied.

"Let's run through the routine again," her coach said. "Take it from the top with the pivot and mohawk sequence. But this time, let's add in a Salchow."

"Sure," said Grace, but she winced at the thought of jumps. She wasn't as comfortable with them as with the rest of her moves.

Grace skated around the edge of the rink, psyching herself up for the jumps. Coach Roberts always had her start with the Salchow. It was the easiest jump. Grace did her turns, then swung her right leg around and spun in the air before landing back on her right leg. Her nerves calmed as she landed.

Coach clapped. "Beautiful!" he called. "Now try a double Salchow."

Grace's eyes grew wide. Sometimes she made the double, but not always. Taking a deep breath, Grace launched into the move. This time, she twirled twice in the air. Her skate caught on the ice when she landed, and she stumbled. Her fingers grazed the ice, but she didn't fall.

"Sorry," she muttered.

"It's okay," Coach Roberts said. "You just need practice. We'll start fresh tomorrow."

Grace frowned. As much as she loved skating, she didn't like making mistakes.

"Cheer up," her coach said. "You had a terrific practice. You'll master the jumps."

Grace nodded. She sat on the bench to take off her skates and heard applause from the next rink. "Fantastic!" Coach Patricia yelled to Lauren.

Grace had been so focused on her own routine that she'd forgotten Lauren was even there. She turned to watch Lauren's moves. The other skater was doing not only single Salchows but doubles as well.

She makes it look so easy, Grace thought.

As she watched, Grace saw Lauren launch herself off the ice again and do another fancy jump.

There's no way my jumps are as good as hers, Grace thought nervously.

"See you tomorrow, Coach," Grace said. She swung her duffel bag over her shoulder.

"Bright and early," he replied. "And don't worry. You'll be fine. We have plenty of time before the competition."

"I know," Grace said. But inside, she wasn't so sure.

Chapter Three

FUN VS. WINNING

At dinner that night, Grace barely touched her food. She pushed the carrots and chicken around on her plate. Her fork scraped noisily across her plate.

Finally, her mom broke the silence. "What's wrong, sweetie?" her mom asked.

"Nothing," Grace said. "It's just that I met this new girl, Lauren, at practice today. She's entering the skating competition, too. And she's really good."

"That's great news," her dad said, smiling. "Maybe you can practice together. It might help you motivate each other."

Grace glared at him. "That's what she said, too," she muttered.

"So what's the problem?" Dad asked.

Grace scowled. "Her jumps are perfect!" she explained. "There's no way I can be that good."

"Hold up a second," said her dad. "You don't know that. Everyone has his or her own strengths. You're a great skater."

"But I'll never be able to do jumps like that," Grace argued.

Her mom shook her head. "Now, honey. I've seen how hard you can work," she said. "When you put your mind to something, you can do it."

"But —" Grace started to say.

"And who says you have to do those kinds of jumps?" her dad interrupted. "You're great at spins. Do more of them."

Grace thought about that. *I am great at spins,* she realized. *But will it be enough to win?*

"And I know you want to win, but didn't we talk about having fun too? Don't forget that," her mom reminded her.

"I know," Grace said. Deep down, she knew her parents were right.

But how can I have fun when I want to win so badly? she wondered.

Chapter Four

LOSING FOCUS

The next morning, Grace's mom woke her up bright and early. "Up and at 'em," Mom said, walking into Grace's room and opening the blinds.

"What time is it?" Grace mumbled. She looked out the window. It was still almost completely dark.

"Six o'clock. You said you wanted to wake up extra early today so you could practice more," her mom reminded her.

Grace rubbed her eyes and sat up. "Be right down," she said, swinging her legs to the floor. *Early mornings are tough,* she thought, *but it will all be worth it in the end.*

Grace got dressed and went downstairs. She grabbed her skating bag and headed out the door. She'd hoped to have the whole rink to herself so she could focus, but when she arrived, Lauren was already there.

"Hey," said Lauren, skating over to Grace. "I guess we both had the same idea. My coach isn't here yet either."

Grace looked down and focused on lacing up her skates. She didn't want to talk to Lauren. All she wanted to do was practice. "I have a lot of work to do," she told Lauren, smiling tightly. "See you later."

"Sounds good!" Lauren said. She turned and skated away to practice.

Why is she being so nice? Grace wondered. She pushed the thought out of her head and turned on her music.

Grace stepped onto the ice and started her warm-up. She quickly ran through the glides, swizzles, and spins. They were flawless. Grace breathed a sigh of relief. *At least I have those down,* she thought.

Next she readied herself for the jumps. The single Salchow went off without a hitch. Grace took a deep breath. Time for the double Salchow.

She pushed off from her left foot and leaped into the air. Tucking her arms in close to her body, Grace spun twice in the air and landed back on the ice on her right foot. She stumbled slightly on the landing, but her hands didn't touch the ice.

"Much better!" she heard Coach Roberts call from the side of the rink.

"Thanks," Grace said.

"I'm glad you're here so early," her coach said. "I know jumps aren't your favorite, so I was thinking we could add more spins to your routine. They're your strength, and I want you to be comfortable."

"Works for me," Grace said. *If it were up to me, I'd only be doing spins,* she thought.

"Let's take it from the top," Coach Roberts said. "This time, I'd like to see a camel spin. Then take that into the catch foot camel."

"No problem," said Grace. She skated to the center of the ice. The glides and crossovers came easily. Then it was time for the camel spin.

She raised her right leg into the air and made sure her knee was higher than her hip as she glided across the ice. For the catch foot, Grace grabbed her raised foot and pulled it to her head. She spun easily on the ice.

For the next twenty minutes, Grace worked on her routine. She practiced her jumps and barely wobbled on her landings. She spun effortlessly. But then she made the mistake of looking at Lauren's rink. Her jumps were perfect. She even did a flip jump, easily rotating a full turn in the air.

Grace scowled. When she had tried that jump, she'd almost twisted her ankle. Her good mood started to disappear.

Coach Roberts immediately noticed. "We still have forty-five minutes left of practice," he said. "Stay focused."

Grace nodded. She sped across the ice with her arms open wide. When the music slowed, she did her camel spin on cue. She moved to do the catch foot, but as she did, she caught a glimpse of Lauren out of the corner of her eye. Grace immediately lost her footing and stumbled.

"Grace, focus!" her coach yelled again.

"I'm trying," she mumbled. But even as she said it, her eyes followed Lauren's perfect jumps.

Coach Roberts looked irritated. "Let's take it from the beginning," he said.

Grace got into position and started again. She wanted to do well. She pulled her arms in tight to get extra speed on her spins, but Lauren's music was stuck in her head. When it came time for the Salchow, Grace tripped on the ice.

"Let's call it a day," said Coach Roberts.

They couldn't be done already! "But we have thirty minutes to go," Grace said, looking at the clock.

"There's no point in practicing for another thirty minutes when your head isn't in it," Coach Roberts said. "We'll try again tomorrow."

Grace opened her mouth to argue, but she knew her coach was right. She slumped her shoulders and skated to the bench to change out of her skates.

Grace grabbed her duffel and headed for the door. Out of the corner of her eye, she saw Lauren watching her. Grace turned away. When she turned back, Lauren was focused on her routine again. Just like Grace should have been.

Chapter Five

AN UNWELCOME OFFER

Two days later, Grace still couldn't seem to focus. She sat in the school cafeteria and picked at her sandwich while her friends talked about the River City Winter Festival. Grace would have joined in, but she was too distracted.

What's the point of competing when Lauren is so much better than I am? she thought.

"Hey," someone said, sitting down beside her. "Can I talk to you a second?"

Grace looked up and saw Lauren. "I guess," she said, shrugging. *It's not like I'm doing anything besides feeling sorry for myself,* she thought.

"I've been watching you on the ice," said Lauren.

Grace looked at her in surprise. *Why was Lauren watching me?* she wondered. *To see how much better she is?*

"So?" Grace said.

"I noticed that you were having trouble with a couple of your jumps the other day. I think I might be able to help," Lauren said.

"Why would you want to help me?" Grace snapped.

"I just thought I could give you some tips, and you —" began Lauren.

"I don't need tips from you," Grace interrupted.

Lauren looked surprised at Grace's tone. "I didn't mean —" she started to say.

"Forget it," said Grace. She picked up what was left of her sandwich and walked out of the cafeteria.

It's bad enough I have to see how much better she is on the ice, Grace thought. *I don't need her gloating at school, too.*

* * *

Coach Roberts could tell something was bothering Grace as soon as she arrived at practice that afternoon. "What's with the long face?" he asked.

"Lauren stopped by my table at lunch today," Grace told him. "She wanted to rub in how much better than me she is."

As she spoke, Grace grabbed her skates from her bag and angrily tugged them on.

Her coach frowned. "Really?" he said. "That doesn't sound like Lauren at all."

Grace tugged on her laces and one snapped. "Shoot!" she said. "Nothing is going right today."

"Maybe this isn't a good day to practice," Coach Roberts said.

Grace's eyes stung with tears. "You think I can't do it," she said. "Just like Lauren."

Coach Roberts sat next to Grace on the bench. "I know you can do it. You're the only one who seems to think you can't," he said. "You psyched yourself out from the moment you met Lauren. Patricia told me Lauren thought she could help you with jumps, and —"

Grace shook her head. "I don't want her help," she insisted, wiping away her tears. "I don't need it."

Coach Roberts sighed. "You used to love skating," he said. "You need to get that back. Take a few days off. Make sure this competition is something you still want to do. Don't come back to the ice until you know if you even want to skate again."

Grace wanted to tell Coach Roberts she couldn't afford to take time off. She didn't need the time off. But she could tell from his expression that he wasn't going to budge. Instead, she slung her duffel bag over her shoulder and walked toward the door.

But as she walked out of the rink, Grace realized Coach Roberts was right. At the moment, she didn't want to skate at all.

Chapter Six

KNOWING WHAT YOU WANT

Grace spent the next few days moping. She hid the duffel bag that held her skates in her closet so she wouldn't have to think about skating. In school, she couldn't focus and avoided Lauren.

After school one afternoon, Grace looked over at the closet door her duffel bag was hidden behind. She thought about the skating gear stored inside. She did barefoot crossovers on her carpet and missed the feel of her skates.

Grace tried pushing away thoughts of skating, but it was no use. Skating was what she loved to do. It made her happy. She didn't want to give it up.

At dinner that night, she explained the situation to her parents. "What should I do?" she asked.

"Grace, this isn't our decision to make," her dad said. "What do you think you should do?"

Grace pushed the food around on her plate. "I miss it," she said.

"Well, then, that's your answer," said Grace's mom.

"But what about Lauren?" Grace asked.

"What about her?" her dad replied. "I thought you said she offered to help."

"That's what she said," Grace said slowly. But she wondered if Lauren could have really meant it.

Why would she want to help me? Grace wondered. *I'm her competition.*

"Besides," said her mom, "you need to think about what you want. It doesn't matter what anyone else is doing."

Grace nodded. She knew her parents were right. It sounded just like what Coach Roberts had told her. "Then I know what I want," she said. "It's what I have always wanted. To skate."

Chapter Seven

A GREAT IDEA

Coach Roberts was waiting for Grace when she arrived at the rink the next day. "I was hoping you'd come to this decision," he said. "I added more spins to the routine to make it more fun. You up for it?"

"Definitely," said Grace. She looked to the next rink and saw Lauren practicing. She tried to push her worries out of her head. She thought about what her mom said. *It's about what I want, not about anyone else,* she reminded herself.

"From the top," Coach Roberts said as he turned on the music.

Grace skated across the ice, crossing her ankles in time to her music. She aced the camel spin and even nailed the Salchow.

"That's the Grace I know!" Coach Roberts shouted above the music.

Grace grinned. It felt good to be back on her game. She'd missed skating like this. She did the catch foot camel spin, and Coach Roberts clapped.

"Let's try the two extra spins now," her coach called across the ice. "We haven't done them in a while, but I'm sure you'll be fine. The first is a sit spin, and the second is the layback spin. The most important thing in these spins is centering. Find a spot to focus on so you don't get dizzy."

Grace let the music fill her head and told herself to center. She skated back to the center of the ice, gaining momentum for the sit spin. Then she crouched low, almost touching the ice. She raised her right foot off the ground and spun with her arms extended in front of her.

"Very nice," Coach Roberts called. "Now the layback."

Grace nodded. This time, she started upright. She bent her right leg high behind her. She arched her back and lowered her head back so it looked like it was reaching for the skate.

When she finished, she heard applause again, but when she glanced over at the edge of the rink, it wasn't just Coach Roberts standing there. Lauren was with him. Grace's body stiffened.

"You do great spins," said Lauren.

Grace searched Lauren's face to see if the other girl was making fun of her, but she only saw encouragement in Lauren's eyes.

"Thanks," said Grace. She shuffled back and forth on her skates. "Your jumps are amazing," she finally said.

"Thank you!" said Lauren. "If we could just put the two of us together, we'd win the competition for sure."

Grace saw Coach Roberts and Coach Patricia exchange looks.

"Now that's a great idea," said Coach Roberts.

Chapter Eight

PAIRING UP

Grace flew through her front door after practice. She couldn't wait to tell her parents about Coach Roberts's great idea.

"Well, this is a nice change," Grace's dad said when he saw her smiling face. "Did Lauren miss a jump or something?"

"Dad!" Grace said at the same time her mom hollered, "Frank!"

"Kidding! Kidding!" her dad said, laughing. "What's up?"

"Coach Roberts thought both Lauren and I could win the competition," she explained. "There's nothing in the rules that says we can't do a joint routine. With Lauren's great jumps and my awesome spins, there's no way we'd lose."

Grace's mom and dad grinned. "Teamwork. Imagine that," Grace's mom said with a smile.

Grace blushed. "I know I've been kind of a pain," she said. "I forgot why I started skating to begin with. I just got so jealous. Lauren really wanted us to help each other. That's why she offered to help me with the jumps."

"We're glad you're back on track," her dad said, "and that you girls found a way to work things out."

"Now, I have to build up my strength. What's for dinner?" said Grace.

"Broccoli, chicken, rice, and salad," Grace's mom answered.

"Great! I'll have double portions of everything," said Grace. She already couldn't wait to get back to the rink. She knew she and Lauren were going to tear up the ice.

Chapter Nine

TWO HEADS ARE BETTER THAN ONE

Grace and Lauren practiced together every morning and afternoon for a week. Coach Roberts was right. Having them work together showcased both of their best skills.

Grace wasn't jealous of Lauren anymore. She was grateful for Lauren's tips, and glad she could teach Lauren something too.

The day of the competition, Grace arrived at the rink a few minutes early. Lauren came running in at the same time.

"Hi!" said Grace, smiling at her new friend. She couldn't believe that just a few weeks ago she hadn't wanted to talk to Lauren at all.

"Hi!" Lauren greeted her. "Are you nervous?"

Grace thought about all their practices and how far she'd come. She thought about how great skating with Lauren was. "Nope," she said.

"Me neither!" Lauren said happily. "Didn't I tell you we'd motivate each other?"

"Did you say that?" Grace asked, laughing.

They ran through their routine one last time before the competition. Everything went off without a hitch.

"We nailed it!" Grace said happily. "That was perfect!"

Lauren smiled. "Yeah, we did!" she said. "If we do it the same way in the competition, we'll knock everyone's socks off."

"Or skates," Grace said, giggling.

Chapter Ten

WORKING AS A TEAM

As she waited for the competition to start, Grace scanned the crowd for her parents. She spotted them in the first row. They waved and gave her a thumbs-up.

Grace watched nervously as the first competitor took the ice. "She's really good," Grace said as the skater glided across the rink. She performed a variety of jumps and spins.

"Definitely, but your spins are harder," Lauren said. "And she wobbled a little on the jumps."

Finally, it was their turn to skate. Coach Roberts and Patricia both wished them luck, and Grace and Lauren took their places on the ice.

When the music started, Grace did her mohawk sequence while Lauren performed a jump combination. The girls glided across the ice and performed swizzles and crossovers.

Then Grace broke away to do her catch camel and sit spin. She had been practicing her Salchows all week with Lauren's help. She knew she could do it. Grace flew into the air for a double Salchow and landed effortlessly.

Lauren went into the Axel. It was the hardest jump of their routine, and Grace couldn't do it. Lauren pushed herself off the ice with her right foot. She rotated one and a half turns in the air before landing on her left foot. It was perfect.

The crowd cheered as their routine came to an end. Grace and Lauren grinned at each other as they skated off the ice to wait for the results.

"That was great, girls!" Coach Roberts said as they sat down to watch the other competitors.

When the last skater finished, everyone waited for the judges' scores. The results could not come fast enough.

"I'm so nervous," Grace whispered to Lauren.

"We did the best we could," Lauren said.

The crowd grew quiet as the head judge stepped up to the microphone. "First, I'd like to congratulate all of our skaters on their wonderful performances," he said. "You were all great. And, now, the results you've been waiting for."

Grace squeezed Lauren's hand as the judge read off the names of the second- and third-place winners. The crowd cheered as the skaters accepted their medals.

The judged cleared his throat as he got ready to announce first place. "First place goes to a unique routine that included not only a high level of difficulty, but also the ability to work together as a team," the judge said. "Congratulations to Grace White and Lauren Smith! Girls, please come up and accept your medals."

Grace squealed. She and Lauren jumped up and hugged before running up to get their medals.

"I already know what I'll be doing for next year's competition," Grace said, smiling at Lauren.

"Oh, yeah?" Lauren asked.

"Yep. An Axel," Grace said. "And I'm going to need my teammate to help make it happen."

AUTHOR BIO

Margaret Gurevich has wanted to be a writer since second grade. She has written for many magazines and currently writes young adult and middle grade books. She lives with her husband, son, and two furry kitties.

ILLUSTRATOR BIO

Katie Wood fell in love with drawing when she was very small. Since graduating from Loughborough University School of Art and Design in 2004, she has been living her dream working as a freelance illustrator. From her studio in Leicester, England, she creates bright and lively illustrations for books and magazines all over the world.

GLOSSARY

competition (kom-puh-TISH-uhn) — a contest of some kind

dedicated (DED-i-kay-tid) — fully committed to something

exhibition (ek-suh-BISH-uhn) — a public display

motivate (MOH-tuh-vate) — to encourage someone to do something

patience (PAY-shuhnss) — the ability to put up with problems and delays without getting angry or upset

pivoted (PIV-uht-id) — turned suddenly in a different direction

routine (roo-TEEN) — a set of moves a skater performs

sequence (SEE-kwuhnss) — the following of one thing after another in a fixed order

DISCUSSION QUESTIONS

1. Talk about how the relationship between Grace and Lauren changed from the beginning of this story to the end.

2. Why does Grace's coach tell her to take a few days off from skating? Do you think he made the right decision? Talk about your answer.

3. Why is Grace so reluctant to let Lauren help her? Talk about how you would have behaved if you were Grace.

WRITING PROMPTS

1. Have you ever had a rival when it comes to sports or something else? Write about what happened and how you resolved things.

2. Grace's first impression of Lauren isn't a good one. Write about a time your first impression of someone was different from what that person was actually like.

3. Write about Grace and Lauren's first meeting from Lauren's point of view. How do you think it was different? How was it the same?

FAMOUS FEMALE FIGURE SKATERS

Dorothy Hamill: Known as "America's Sweetheart," Dorothy Hamill began figure skating on a pond behind her grandparents' house when she was eight years old. During her career, Hamill was known for her graceful jumps and excellent technical skating abilities. In 1976, she took home the gold medal for figure skating in the XII Winter Olympic games in Austria and went on to become the most sought-after skater in history.

Oksana Baiul: When she received a pair of ice skates for her fourth birthday, it was the beginning of a career for Olympic champion Oksana Baiul. Born in the Ukraine in 1977, Bauil showed talent as a young skater. She started competing by the time she was seven years old. She went on to win the World Figure Skating Championships in 1993, when she was just fifteen years old, and took home Olympic gold in the 1994 Winter Olympic Games at the age of sixteen.